Write your name here!

This book belongs to:

_____

_____

My Teddy Bear is called:

_____

North Parade
Publishing Ltd

©2022 North Parade Publishing Ltd.
3-6 Henrietta Mews,
Bath BA2 6LR. UK
Printed in China.

The Teddy Bear Secret

Illustrated by **Gail Yerril**

Once upon a time there lived
a bear called Bear.

He had fuzzy brown fur, and a beetle black nose, and a person called Ben.

Ben thought Bear was the best teddy bear in the whole wide world, but of course, all teddies are special, particularly when they're yours.

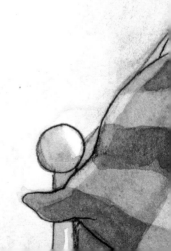

Everybody thought that Ben looked after Bear.

No-one could have guessed (least of all Ben!), that really, it was the other way around.

Bear kept sharks out of the water when Mum went to fetch Ben for his bath...

He fought the monsters under
the bed while Ben slept...

...and he whispered happy thoughts in his ear, so all his dreams were good.

You might not know it, but your teddy bear does all these things for you, too, and even more besides!

Teddy bears all over the world take care of their people every single day, without anybody ever guessing, and all because of the Teddy Bear Secret.

Whenever there's a person nearby, bears have to keep very still and quiet.

But when they're on their own, or when you're fast asleep, you can be sure that your teddy bear is a very busy bear indeed!

Ben's Bear had a very important job in the playroom, warning all the other toys whenever there was a person nearby.

"Everybody go teddy!"

he would shout, and all the bears would stop whatever they were doing...

...Climbing up the curtains...

...or sliding down them...

...holding tea parties...

...and teddy bears' picnics...

...riding on spinning tops...

...or encouraging the toy soldiers not to fall out with one another...

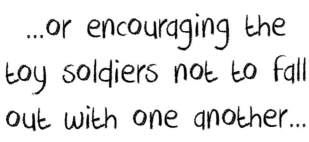

...and sit perfectly still wherever they happened to be.

That's why you might not always be able to find your teddy where you left him, (bears are terribly good at hide and seek!)...

...and why you might lose things from time to time...

...like coloured pencils...

...favourite books...

...indoor shoes...

...and outdoor boots...

The next time you lose your pencil sharpener, be sure to talk to your teddy about it, because I expect he has been using it.

Just remember, he might not be able to tell you where it is, because of the Teddy Bear Secret...

...but that's why bears make the best listeners, after all!

So cuddle your bear, and kiss him goodnight; for while he is with you, the bedbugs won't bite!

Goodnight, Teddy!